IGNÁT HERRMANN

Childless

.

Contents

A VERY SHORT INTRODUCTION

Ignát Herrmann was born in Chotěboř, part of the historical land of Bohemia, in 1854, the thirteenth child of large family. As a young man he moved to Prague where he worked as a baker's apprentice, a travelling salesman, law clerk, bank clerk, reporter and as editor of the satirical magazine, *Švanda dudák*, which he also founded.

He wrote several novels, and hundreds of short stories, most of which were set in and around Prague and described the city and the people that he witnessed in his daily life.

He died in 1935.

ONE

I van Hron been married for ten years; he had a beautiful wife and was rich. Even his most intimate friends said, not without a touch of envy, that he had "a first-rate berth." They might indeed envy him, for Ivan Hron seemed a spoilt child of fortune. When he had left school, he had entered the university to study law, in order to take his degree. This he did chiefly because his father, a well-to-do tradesmen in the country, wished it; he wanted his son to rise in the world. And the son did as his father wished and went to college. But he did not finish his university career. As a young hothead he had been mixed up in some political propaganda; the affair had at first earned him several weeks' arrest, then he was sent down. Although his indiscretion had been of a purely political character, the academic senate wished to keep the reputation of the university unstained, and departed for good with the ill-advised youth. This outcome of his folly had so roused his father's anger that he ordered him out of the house and disinherited him. These things will happen! For whom does a father work and worry from morning till night, if not for his children? What right had a foolish boy, dependent on his father, to spoil his whole future by one careless act?

That Ivan Hron had spoilt his, was his father's firm conviction, and he succeeded in convincing his mother too. With this conviction old Hron died.

And Ivan? When he was in these desperate straits, he knocked at the doors of a Great Bank where clerks were wanted. He obtained work, and dedicated his mind and body to the concern for the salary of thirty florins. It was not long before his superiors found out that he had not wasted his time at the public school where he had spent the greater part of his life, nor during the two years at the university when studying law. Evidently he had after all not entirely spoilt his future outlook. His immediate superiors recommended him to the higher authorities as an eminently "useful" young man, and Ivan Hron got preferment. But his humbler colleagues had no idea of the surprise which was in store for them when after a few years the general manager died. While the cashiers, head clerks, accountants, and other employees, formerly of a very superior rank to Hron's, remained at their desks or marble counters, Ivan, who had assisted very successfully in some important transactions, was unexpectedly called in at the board meeting, where the chairman proceeded to deliver an impressive address, full of oratorical flourishes which befitted the occasion, and asked him whether he would be willing to accept the vacant post.

"We have the greatest confidence in you," he concluded.

Although Ivan Hron was exceedingly astonished, he showed his surprise in no way. Up to a certain point he had confidence in his own ability, and presence of mind enough to answer that his acceptance would depend on their conditions.

"The conditions will be the same that held good for your predecessor," said the chairman of the board meeting, "and if you fulfil our expectations they will be better still. The state of our affairs entitles us to great hopes; we only need a firm, energetic director. That is why we have chosen you."

Ivan Hron accepted, and the evening papers carried the news that same day to all those who were interested in the appointment of the general manager.

"Lucky fellow!" some said. "They'll have a good head on their shoulders," said others.

A most promising future now lay before Ivan Hron. He remained unmarried for another year, as though to test the ground under his feet. And when he found it was firm, he got married.

Many people were surprised that he had chosen a wife without a fortune. They were still more surprised when they heard that she had been an heiress until lately, when with the failure of her father's business the glamour which surrounded her had suddenly been eclipsed. Why had he knocked at that door when his position made him worth thousands? Was he under an obligation to her? Had he wooed her earlier and was now going to redeem his promises as a man of honour should? When circumstances take such a turn as his had done, surely promises are no longer binding, and so-called honour in these cases was ridiculous, said the more experienced and worldly among his friends and acquaintances.

Nobody knew that this unpromising match had cost Ivan Hron a great deal of trouble and perseverance; that he looked upon the father's failure as a happy coincidence; that the girl had yielded to the urgent request of her parents to accept the hand which was offering her a safe future, and which might perhaps save the whole family from the greatest misery. And Ivan Hron had beamed with happiness although he had led his pale bride to the altar and out of the church in and almost fainting condition.

He had now been married ten years. He was a handsome man in the forties, and some of his former fellow-students, now elderly clerks in lawyers' offices, unbriefed barristers, or doctors who had failed in their final examinations, looked with envy on the former student who had not finished his university career because he had been sent down.

Many of them were married and had several children; their wives had aged before their time, and often there was hardly enough for the current household expenses. Ivan Hron meanwhile belonged to the "elite." He had his carriage, was rarely seen on foot; his wife was still a beautiful woman, his salary increased from year to year; he lived in his own handsome villa, travelled for six weeks in the year, and had no children.

No children! His friends did not know how painful this part of his good fortune was to Hron. For none of the successes and attainments of his life gave him the happiness which a wicker-basket with muslin curtains and the downy head of a rosy, beloved small creature asleep in it would have given him. In spite of all the glamour of his brilliant, exciting life, Hron did not get rid of the old-fashioned feeling that life is perfect only when it is blessed with children. What point, what aim was there in his whole successful career? Why had he worked himself up to the highest position which was open to him, why did he save, to whom would he leave his fortune when, old and frail, he would end his days? What would rejoice his heart in old age?

Moreover, in his case his disappointment was not one of the accidents of life; he did not count how many years he had been married to his beloved Magda and still they were alone. He had married on purpose to have a family, and therefore this

5

unfulfilled desire hurt him all the more. He had been bred in the country and was untouched by the town-bred egoism which aims solely at enjoyment for its own sake, at an untroubled existence dedicated to the "Ego" and its wishes. He wanted children, and when he took his beloved bride home he looked forward to holding a little creature in his arms in course of time. Perhaps the full measure of his longing for a family was due to his having early been disowned by his own people on account of his youthful folly; he had never been received again under the paternal roof. He longed to fill up this void by his marriage to Magdalena. He watched her looks, almost spied upon her sighs at night, and trembled with impatience for the moment when she would blushingly confide to him her sweetest secret but this moment never came. She confided nothing; she went to and fro in their beautifully furnished home, and her face more and more distinctly took on a sad, almost pained expression; a line appeared which started from her prettily shaped nose and included her lips. This expression did not even quite vanish when she laughed heartily; and when she was not smiling, the wistful, sorrowful look quite gained the upper hand.

Was she too feeling what it was that made them miss being perfectly happy? Did she know what was passing in her husband's soul? How could she fail to feel and to guess? No one is so absolutely the slave of his will at every moment, that not a word or a look should betray what is slumbering in the depth of his heart, or what it is for which he is hungering and thirsting. Ivan Hron was no exception to the rule. There was hardly a moment when Mrs Hron did not guess her husband's wishes, if guessing indeed were necessary. Was she not a woman?

Hron would often invite friends to dinner or supper so as to have life in his empty, quiet rooms, and to see them a little untidy. There were times when he did not feel happy in the spotless surroundings of his home, where for months together everything stood in its appointed place, polished, and shining with neatness; where not a speck of dust was to be found, and the well-swept carpets hushed every footstep; where sounds of romping were never heard.

"You are living like a prince," said one of his guests; "how comfortable this house is, and how charmingly furnished."

"And what lovely works of art," added his visitor's wife, who did not get tired of looking again and again at the beautiful pictures and graceful statuettes, or of turning over the leaves of albums filled with photographs of towns and lovely places which Hron either alone or with his wife had visited. She looked at the antique furniture almost with a touch of envy.

"You do know how to arrange things," she sighed; "you are lucky."

Ivan Hron looked round the things which had excited her envy, and looked almost bored. They had interested him chiefly at the time when he bought them; it gave him pleasure to arrange them or put them up on the walls, but after that he got accustomed to them, seeing them every day, and in the end he hardly noticed them. He said without a note of pleasure in his voice, and thinking of the rotund figure of the little woman:

"The rooms are pretty enough, but they are too quiet. I wish there were more of us."

He glanced furtively at his wife who had ceased to smile; he even thought that it was all that Magdalena could do to suppress the tears which were rising to her eyes.

Another time they themselves were on a visit to friends who had three small children; the youngest was a charming, curly boy. They were entertaining them with singing, music, and

7

animated conversation, but none of these things seemed to interest Hron. He devoted himself entirely to the little rascal in his highchair; he took him on his knee, allowed him to pull his nose and beard, chased him again and again under the table and caught him up to begin afresh.

Mrs Hron kept up the appearance of conversation with her hosts, but she was casting perpetual side-glances at her husband's game with the boy, and her eyes betrayed the pain which was wringing her heart. This one gift to him was denied her! How happy she would be if the laughter of children were to echo through their own house, if Ivan could chase a barefooted little fellow of his own!

In the middle of the game Hron suddenly lifted his head and caught one of these glances; he understood what was passing in her mind and left the boy alone. His absorption in the strange child must look like a reproach, and he did not reproach her, he loved her far too much for that. Had they any right, moreover, to reproach each other? Did any one in the world know whose fault it was that they had remained alone? Once he had taken refuge from his secret disappointment in a visit to a doctor, and confided in him. Was there a remedy? What could be done? Whose fault was this misfortune? No, not fault, he corrected himself; there was no fault, no failing… but the cause, the cause?

That was difficult to say. Sometimes it was the husband, sometimes the wife – a physiological problem, inexplicable. Perhaps incompatibility, two natures which do not meet; there was no explanation, no help.

Then Ivan Hron began to brood. He thought over his past life; he was wealthy, without a blemish or taint. He must be unsuitably mated then? Perhaps he had been too hasty about the whole affair.

How many times has he seen his wife before their marriage? Two or three times; first in Dresden on a holiday. He had noticed a gentleman and a charming girl who were talking to each other in Czech. He concluded that they must be his countrymen, probably also on holiday. He had seen her, heard her talking Czech, and fallen in love with her. He had introduced himself and followed them like a shadow for two days; then they had gone home. Soon afterwards he also left; he took no further pleasure in his surroundings. He had learned that the gentleman was a manufacturer from one of the larger towns in Bohemia, the girl was his daughter. After a while he purposely visited the town and ventured to call on the family. He was received with civility – no more. The girl was a distinguished personality, but she was very cold. Her eyes had plainly showed him her astonishment when he presented himself: "Does our accidental meeting in Dresden give you the right to follow me to the bosom of my family?" they seemed to say.

He went away, and a week later boldly asked for her hand. He wrote to her and to her father at the same time. The father's letter was very polite; he evaded the disagreeable duty of a direct answer by the promise that his daughter herself should send a decision.

She had decided. Graciously but firmly she rejected his proposal.

"Well, that's finished," Hron said to himself, "now I must leave it alone. I suppose I am not important enough for her."

But then the unexpected thing had happened: he saw from the newspapers six months later that her father's business had failed.

This news produced a strange sensation in Ivan Hron. He

could have shouted for joy. How would his chances stand now? He returned to the town where they lived to repeat his offer personally.

How embarrassed they had been when he appeared; almost as if they were ashamed of themselves! Hron told them as tactfully as possible that his position would ensure that daughter a life free of cares, and all the comforts she had been used to in her own home.

The girl had seemed almost in despair. This time her father spoke for her. He did not refuse Hron's offer, but asked for a respite: "Wait a month or two… or perhaps six months; have patience," he said. "You do not know how much we have all suffered; everything is changed. And we have to see many things. I know you are a generous man, you have proved it by returning now that we are in trouble. It is not every man who thinks as you do."

Ivan Hron did wait for a whole six months; after that he wrote again, urgently, almost imploringly. It was not the general manager of an important banking combine who spoke in these letters, but a young enthusiast. And Magda became his own. Her father wrote to him that she consented. Then Hron had married her.

Later on he often thought of all this, and of the strange circumstances with which his suit and marriage had been attended. Had not fate in the first instance pointed out his way? Ought he not to have buried his hopes after that first refusal? Perhaps he would have found a girl equally beautiful, gentle and distinguished who would have made him wholly happy…

He was always seized with a feeling of unspeakable sorrow when he arrived at this thought. Had Magda unconsciously had premonitions which had made her stand out against the marriage? Did she guess that she would never make her husband entirely happy? Was it a conviction that she would remain childless?

Then it would be she who was at fault!

Ivan Hron was almost maddened by his pondering and brooding at times. But tenderest compassion and deep pain filled his heart when, sometimes, late at night after having finished some important piece of work, he entered their bedroom on tiptoe. Before opening the door he would listen whether he could hear her sobbing. Then he would wait until the spasms subsided, creep to his bed like a thief, relieved when he heard her breathing quietly, and in the morning when he waked her with a kiss, express in it his whole love and tenderness. And when his wife returned his embrace so warmly and gratefully, she seemed to be asking his forgiveness. When he looked at her as she went about her occupations and duties during the day with care and thoughtfulness, he fell in love with her afresh, and kissed her as on that first day when he had taken her to their new home. Therefore the constant recurrence of the thought: "How much happier we might be if there were yet another being to care for…" was all the more painful to him.

TWO

One beautiful afternoon in the summer Ivan returned home earlier than usual from his office. As he had his own latchkey he had no need to ring the bell, and entered unobserved. He put his hat and stick down in his study, and went towards his wife's room. He did not hear his own step on the thick carpet… Magda had not heard it either.

She hardly had time between the moment of his opening the door and coming up to her, to fold up a letter which she had been reading, and slip it into the envelope. She did it quietly, and Hron did not notice that her hands were trembling. When he was by her side, she leant her left hand with the letter on the table, and smoothed down something in her dress with the right hand, thus keeping both her hands occupied. He could not have failed to feel them trembling if he had touched them.

"You've had a letter?" asked Ivan, pointing to the envelope which peeked out from beneath her fingers; he bent down to kiss her.

Every drop of blood ebbed from her face when her lips met those of her husband; her half-extinguished "Yes" was lost in her kiss.

"From home?" he continued, looking at the stamp, "what news?"

Involuntarily he stretched out his hand for the letter. At that moment Mrs Hron felt as though she must run away or throw herself out of the window... but if she would avoid a catastrophe she must do nothing to rouse his suspicion. Her fingers painfully unclasped, but leant the more heavily on the table.

Hron took up the letter.

"That looks like a weekly review," he said good-humouredly, feeling it with his fingers, "have you read it?" He half pulled the letter from the envelope, and recognised his mother-in-law's handwriting.

"Not quite," answered the young woman. She tried to speak as audibly as she could, but her voice failed her, and her husband began to open the sheets which enclosed another sheet of paper.

"Well, the volumes you write to them are not much shorter," he said kindly, and looked at her before he quite unfolded the letter.

She was standing upright, looking upon his hands with fear in her eyes, and was as white as chalk. Her fixed eyes did not take in her husband's astonishment.

Ivan Hron did not understand; but he thought he did. He suddenly remembered that she never touched his letters, however long they might have been lying on his writing-table: that she never even read a postcard addressed to him; she never showed the least curiosity about his correspondence. He had returned this reticence with regards to her letters. He never touched them without first asking: "May I?" Today he had failed to do this... she had not even finished reading the letter... he had broken the custom which had become a tacit understanding between them. That must be the cause of her astonishment and consternation. Therefore Ivan Hron folded the sheet up again,

13

put it back in the envelope which he laid down on the table, and said in a conciliatory tone: "Forgive me, Magda, that was not right."

His wife forced herself to a gentle smile to conceal her terror, and it was a little while before she was able to say: "You know it is from our people, nothing of importance, nothing new."

She at once turned the conversation: "You are early today; has anything happened?"

"What should have happened?" said her husband, "I hurried home because I hoped we might get a walk. It is such lovely weather. If you feel inclined, we might go to the Sofia Island. Will you get ready?"

Whistling softly to himself, he went to his room to wash his hands and put on fresh cuffs.

When he had gone, his wife opened a drawer of her bureau which contained her most precious and valuable possessions, took out a small box of cedar wood, locked the letter up in it, put the key in her pocket and went out to dress.

They went down the staircase together and out into the street, where Hron offered his arm to his wife. He was delighted to feel how firmly she put her hand on his arm and pressed close to him. Yes, this arm was her hold and firm protection in this world!

Ivan Hron had no idea of what was passing in her mind.

A few days after this incident, which had passed entirely from Hron's memory, he was left alone in the house. He was planning his annual holiday outside Bohemia with his wife, and according to their custom Magda always went home to her parents for a few days first. They were now old and she wished to see them and have the satisfaction of having been with them once more.

14

In her absence Ivan made preparations for their departure. His leave had begun already, and he spent his days at home. He locked up things that were to be left behind, and put everything in order. The next day Mrs Hron was to return from her native town.

Ivan Hron came home from his dinner at a restaurant, and began to pack his handbag. Then he went through all the rooms to see whether he had forgotten anything. He went into his wife's room, and smiled, noticing the order and neatness of everything.

Suddenly his eye was caught by her walnut bureau. All the drawers were locked except the top one which had been pushed back hastily.

"Just fancy, all her treasures unlocked," he thought: "the room is not locked either; the servant might have put her nose into everything."

Involuntarily and without a set purpose, he took hold of the two ornamental bronze rings and pulled out the drawer.

In it were books, jewellery, embroideries, photographs, and keepsakes. A box of cedar-wood was in the right-hand corner. He knew it; he himself had given it to her as a Christmas or New Year's present, when she had expressed a wish for a box in which to keep various trifles.

Hron touched the little box, and noticed that the key of wrought iron was in it.

"Careless little woman! The drawer open and the key in her box! And what about all those sacred secrets, those valueless, and yet so carefully guarded mysteries?"

It suddenly struck him, although he did not feel the ordinary human curiosity: "I wonder what they are, these things that my dear Magda has collected in this box?"

15

He almost smiled at the thought that perhaps his first letter was among them, the one which she had answered with a refusal? As though this thought had with lightning-speed been transferred to his hand, he touched the key, turned it and opened the lid. The remembrance of the letter, the answer to which had poisoned six months of his life, was now really exciting his curiosity. Had Magda kept it? He himself was keeping her answer in a drawer of his writing-table. Tactless or not... he wanted to know! The little box was filled with receipts and papers of various kinds; on the top was the letter which he had recently held in his hand and returned to his wife. He recognised it by the handwriting and the date on the postmark. But the letter had not been entirely slipped into the envelope, a corner of it was peeping out; Magda had probably read it several times, and put it back loosely. Another letter was folded into the large sheets which were covered with his mother-in-law's handwriting, well known to him. Hron could only see the endings of words which were written in an unknown, undeveloped hand.

He did not know why he did it, as he was in fact looking for something else, but he pulled out the sheet which was covered on all its four pages with sprawling, large letters. It was the attempt of a hand still awkward, and not much used to writing fluently. In regular letters... the difference of thickness in the up- and down-strokes carefully observed... only children write like that. Which of the relatives...?

He opened the sheet and read:

"My beloved Mummy, – How good of you to let me write to you again. I would like to write to you every day to tell you that I think of you and pray for you, because the clergyman tells

us at school that we must pray for our parents. But I cannot
pray for Papa who is dead, I pray for my dear Mama whom I
love so much, and I wish she were with me, because I cannot be
with her. I do not know why I cannot be with her, when every
daughter is with her mother. I know I cannot be with my Papa
when he is dead, but why not with my Mama? And when you
say you love me, why do you not take me with you? When I
asked the lady, she tells me that the gentleman would not like
it. What gentleman would not like it? I think you must be in
service like other mothers, and so you cannot have me with
you, and I am so sorry I do not know where you are either. My
beloved Mummy, I would hide in a corner and keep quite quiet,
so as not to worry the gentleman, and all day long I would not
come out of my corner and the gentleman need not see me, and
would not scold you, because he would not know I was there.
But at night, when you go to your little room I would kiss you,
and sleep in your bed, and pray for you and your gentleman as
I do now. I could go to school, the same as I do here, and you
should be pleased with me, for I like my lessons, and I am going
to be moved to a higher standard again. Oh my beloved mother,
I should so like to have a photo of you; the lady has photos of
her sisters and aunts and other relations. When the other lady
came, who is my grandmother, I asked her for one, but she said
I could not have it, because you had not got one. And she told
me I must be good, or else I must never write to you or see you
again. I cried very much, because I only see you once a year, and
then I would never see you at all. My grandmother too cried,
and said I might write to you again, that you had allowed it, and
grandmother will come for this letter and send it to you, for
little girls cannot send letters off by themselves, grandmother
says.

"Dearest Mummy, come again, and come and see me on my birthday, which is on the feast of St. Peter and St. Paul; I shall be eleven. I kiss your hand and am your obedient daughter, Magda.

"*June 15th*."

Ivan Hron had read the letter thinking that it must have got by mistake into the envelope which bore his wife's address. But when he arrived at the signature "Magda," he started. His heart beat with the sudden shock. He felt an unusual wave of heat mount to his head and flood his cheeks. A thought struck him which was so strange that he was startled afresh, and tried not to finish it. He quickly took up the second letter in his mother-in-law's handwriting. He devoured its contents, and large drops of perspiration were standing on his forehead, as though he were running a race. He felt his feet giving way beneath him, and sat down to finish the letter. There was nothing suspicious in it, the usual home news, good advice, enquiries, remembrances to her husband and thanks for his last contribution to household expenses. Only quite at the end: "I am sending you this letter which you will like to see, and am your loving mother..."

There it was! That was the reference to the letter!

Ivan Hron wiped his forehead and read his mother-in-law's letter again, and then that of little eleven-years-old Magda. His wife's name!

He re-read it with the utmost attention.

Now, alas! He understood; he also felt as though his head would burst. His Magda, his wife is little Magda's... impossible!

He sprang to his feet, caught up the little box, and went to his room with it. He locked the door, so as not to be disturbed, and hastily turned out the contents: letters, photographs, empty envelopes. But in spite of his eagerness he was careful to put them down in the proper order, so that nothing should betray afterwards that he had read anything. He felt like a criminal while he was following up Magda's secret. But even if it should be a crime, he was going to commit it!

His hands were trembling feverishly, as he went through the papers; he took all his father- and mother-in-law's letters out of their envelopes, read them at a glance... nothing, nothing! Suddenly he came upon another letter written in the sprawling hand... a second... a third.

There were no more. The one which he had read first was the longest. The others were the more unlettered the older their date. Hron understood; as she made great progress at school she was the more able to express her thoughts; her letters became longer, more legible, more appealing. From each of the four letters spoke the longing of this unknown child to see her mother, to be with her always. This incoherent babbling, these laboured sentences were the expression of a homesick child, praying for the fulfilment of its dearest wish.

Hron sat quite still and reflected painfully; his thoughts were like red-hot wires that penetrated his brain. "My Magda... my Magda!" recurred over and over in his reflections, "and then this child, this second Magda..."

He recalled the moment when he had seen Magda for the first time, remembered how he had wooed her and been refused, and finally accepted. What had happened between the moment when he had first met her and the day when he had at last taken her to his home?

And suddenly Hron turned to his wife's little box again. Did it contain nothing else? Would he find the explanation of this terrible calamity? He remembered that the salesman had drawn

19

his attention to the double bottom when he had bought the box; he had forgotten the contrivance, but now he tried hastily to discover the little hiding-place. He removed the sides, pulled out two ornamental rosettes and… there was the bottom. In it were some faded papers, covered with writing… in Magda's hand. They looked like the beginnings of letters, or notes from a diary; loose leaves, torn out of a book.

Hron began to read these sheets; the handwriting varied considerably, they had evidently been written at odd moments on various occasions. He read, and almost forgot to breathe. These leaves were the outpourings and anguished cries of a woman's soul in despair. If he had had any doubt as to the relationship of the two Magdas, these lines removed them. He saw the whole situation clearly… What a fearful discovery! His own, his adored Magda!

Some of the sheets were quite fragmentary: "There are worse things than death," began one, "and I am on the rack. Everything that I possessed in life has been destroyed… our good name, my father's position after a life of hard work… all in one blow. The fruits of his labour are lost. But, terrible as these losses are – all the more because of their suddenness – they do not shatter me. I wish they did.

"But my fate is more terrible than this; that of my parents is it crowning disaster. The shame, oh the shame! Never-ending shame clings to my wasted life!

"It was all like a horrible, fantastic dream: but the crying of the little creature whom they have separated from me, the crying that I heard for a moment only, which was lost in the distance when they carried the little girl away, this crying was the proof of a dreadful reality.

"And Robert does not return! He has disappeared, and gives

no sign of whether he is alive or dead. Alas! my fall should have helped him to rise, but then came my father's failure… and what can be my value now? Did ever two more terrible misfortunes meet?"

Another sheet began:

"He does not return. Perhaps he is seeking death, perhaps he may have found it. The misery of it! He is a coward; it would have needed energy on his part to begin life afresh, and his life would have given me back my life also. What a fate, to have been betrayed by a mountebank! But the most terrible thing about it is that that other man who came into my life, is again offering me his hand and asking for mine. I am in despair. I resist all I can, but there is my father, who is looking so ill; he does not say anything, but his dear old eyes make such an eloquent appeal… my mother was on her knees before me, wringing her hands and entreating me: Don't refuse him… consent!

"This other, good, honest man is to be deceived. My parents entreat me that it should be so. Shall I give in to their appeal? Shall I make up my mind to hide from him what sort of a wife he wishes to marry?

"And to be separated for ever from that innocent creature… disavow her for ever! For she will not die, I am sure my parents are praying that she might be taken, but my prayers are stronger, and she will live! I keep on praying that she will live…"

Again on another sheet:

"The decision has been made; my conscience has tormented me from the moment when my father said 'Yes' for me. Do I care for him? Have I a right to say I love the man whom I approach with a lie? How can I bear his eyes, how shall I breathe in his embraces?

"They have tormented me, forced my hands! They took away

my child, I do not know where she is. I want to see her… I am dying with longing to kiss her, press her to my heart… where is she?

"They promised that I should see her if I consented to marry him. My child, what a price to pay for your kisses! Unfortunate Ivan! What a price for you to pay for me… how you are being deceived…"

On the last sheet, on which the first lines had been crossed out, he read:

"Tomorrow is my wedding day… I feel as though it were my funeral. Alas! I feel something is being carried to its grave… I myself am burying it. I am murdering my peace of mind… perhaps I am also murdering Ivan's happiness.

"And my father and mother kiss me and embrace me. Neither of them says a word about it, but their eyes are saying a great deal. They are grateful to me that I have yielded, that I have consented to… sell myself. I cannot express what I feel when I see Ivan, full of love, beaming with happiness because I am to be his…

"There is one thought of comfort in these bitter, desperate hours for which I am thanking heaven: Robert is dead. He has gone out of my life; his shadow will never fall between Ivan and me, he will never come back.

"I do not know if the moment will ever come when I shall bear to say that I love Ivan. I tremble when I think of his asking me whether I love him. And perhaps he will ask me tomorrow… tomorrow! But the thought that that coward is dead is balm to my soul."

THREE

I van Hron had finished the perusal of the papers; he breathed a sigh of relief. After what he had read, this fact that the unknown father of little Magda was no longer alive, was a load off his mind. He was breathing audibly, like a man waking up out of a heavy sleep.

"Whoever he was, he is dead now…"

Ivan Hron stared at the sheets and fragmentary notes in front of him with burning eyes; then he slowly put his elbows on to the table and buried his head in his hands; his soul had been profoundly stirred, and a painful sob broke from his compressed throat. A moment later his whole body, his shoulders and hands and head began to tremble, and large tears fell upon the faded, traitorous leaves.

It did not occur to him to think of how long it was since he had cried, nor that he was a strong man with experience of life, and that he ought not to give way; he only felt a fearful scorching pain, such as he had felt once before in his life at the time when he had been banished from his home on account of his ill-considered youthful exploit. But at that time he had been young, and the whole world laid before him. He had then sustained an irreparable loss, but from the depths of his despair he looked for the dawn of a future. What was left to him now?

He was now living that future to which he had been looking forward then; he had climbed to the summit of his life, there was no going higher or further. His daily life was circumscribed, there would be no great changes either in his career or in his home; he had come to the limits of both. He was at the head of his office and he was married; this was the last stage of his life, and though it might go on for another ten or twenty years, it would always be the same. He would get older, one day he would retire; there were no other prospects. He well knew the limits within which he was living, and now, just as he was approaching their border, this thing happened, to poison both the past and the future for him!

Ivan Hron wept for a long time, until his tears naturally ceased to flow. Only now and then convulsive spasms betrayed his inward crying. But even the spasms became less frequent; there was a sob from time to time, and at last a silence.

He sat for a while, supporting his head in his hand. He did not realise how great the relief had been which his tears had given him. When he raised his head, his tears had ceased to flow, only his eyes were a little swollen and inflamed. The expression of his face was calm; the storm had passed. He looked as though he had resigned himself to an irreparable, unalterable fate.

He took his pocket-handkerchief and wiped his eyes; then he quietly replaced the sheets of papers, letters, photographs and trifles in the box in their proper order. Nothing should betray their having been touched by an unauthorised hand. When he took up little Magda's fateful letter, which had so recently caused him the bitterest moment of his life, he glanced once more at the lines written by this unknown, pining little creature. Now he could enter into it much more. Alas! How much bitterness this little heart had already had to taste! But

24

how great must have been the pain that his wife had suffered all the time since she had been tied to him and separated from her child… day by day, whole months, years… ten long years. What fortitude this delicate woman had shown in mastering herself and enduring the separation… or was she upheld by some hope? What was this hope?

Hron stopped short at the words: "Dearest Mummy, come again, come on my birthday, on the day of St. Peter and St. Paul…"

Yes, Magda had complied with her wish. It was a week since she went away, and today was St. Peter and St. Paul. At the moment when her fateful secret had revealed itself to him accidentally, a little creature in some distant place was laughing with joy at her mother's embrace, and his wife was happy in the presence of her growing daughter, answering her thousand questions, asking a thousand herself, kissing her, kissing her for a whole year. But in the midst of all this love and tenderness the clock would strike mercilessly, the day would wane, and Magda press her child closer and yet closer… her child, from whom she must tear herself after a few hours to be separated again for a whole year. And even if she could think of him, her husband, how bitter must that thought be to her! She would have to return to him without betraying by a single word what she had gone through. Her heart would break with the pain of another separation, yet she might not complain; she must master herself with all her strength, so as not to arouse his suspicion. Where would her thoughts be before she returned to him, when he would press her to his heart and kiss her? Every caress which he had taken to himself had really been meant for her little daughter. When she passed her hand over his head she probably thought of her. And perhaps she hoped to win his forgiveness at the moment when he might discover her secret, with the care, tenderness and attention which she had given him. Did she dread that moment? Surely, it must haunt her!

Ivan's heart was caught up in a feeling of unbounded pity. The feeling which was uppermost in his mind was not that he had been deceived, but that he had been excluded from a triple alliance.

Slowly he folded up the letter and put it, and what was left of other things, back into their place, and carried the box to Magda's room. He carefully replaced it in the drawer, which he locked, so that Magda should have no idea that her carelessness had induced any one to open it.

As he left the room, he happened to look into a glass, and noticed his inflamed, swollen eyes. He hurried into his room, poured water into his basin, adding a little lavender water, and sponged and dried his face. When he had done this and brushed his dishevelled hair, Hron slowly changed his clothes. The large, empty rooms seemed lonely, and he felt that he must get away from them into the fresh air, to someplace where he would not be likely to meet many people. He could not bear the idea of seeing any one he knew; he wanted to be alone, to reflect, to work out this problem and come to a resolution. He locked his wife's room and put the key in his pocket, in case the servant should spy upon her secret in his absence. How glad he was that that moment had found him alone; he had allowed the girl to go to a procession. No one had surprised him, no one knew that anything that happened.

He slowly went down the stairs. His thoughts were moving round and round in a strange circle. A picture of Doré's from the *édition de luxe* of his Bible occurred to him; it represented the expulsion from paradise. As he left his house he felt as though he too was being driven from his paradise. Day by day he had hastened hither to meet his beloved Magda. He thought of her return the next day and shivered. How would he feel at meeting her? Would he be able to master his features sufficiently for her not to see that he now knew what she had kept a secret for so long, what perhaps she had meant to keep a secret for ever? What kind of a life between them would it be if Magda discovered *his* secret?

If only he could escape meeting friends today! He wished he were a stranger to all the world.

He went to a part of Prague where he had hardly ever been before, across the "little bridge" and through the passages of the crooked old town on the banks of the Moldavia. It was a fine day; all those who could walk had left the street behind; Hron met only a few strangers. The place seemed almost deserted. He crossed the river by the stone bridge and turned through a side-street towards the Bruska. But that was full of people, so he went through the archway and out into the fields.

He breathed a sigh of relief when he was there, but the consciousness of his sorrow did not leave him. He thought of his wedding-day and his married life. His thoughts came and went incoherently; he thought of the time before his marriage. Who was this man who had been the first to win Magda's heart, her whole heart, even herself? Who was he, the father of Magda, who was dead? When had all that happened? And again he felt the tears rising in his throat, and an immeasurable pain, as though he had lost what he treasured most. But at the time… Magda had not been his! He also thought of the moments when their childlessness had been most bitter to him; when he had looked enviously at his friends' families and their happiness, when he had romped with their children. Now he understood

Magda's mute, eloquent looks on those occasions, which had haunted him. "If that were my child!" she must have thought. Yes: she was thinking of her own child who was living hidden, a stranger among strangers, uncaressed, without a father, and deprived of her mother too during all the years when she most needed her. That was what her looks meant... it was that... that! At moments when Hron had caressed other children her thoughts, with all the suppressed, secret mother-instinct fled to her own lonely little daughter whom she dared not acknowledge, of whom she might not be proud, whom she might not kiss before all the world, nor dress her, nor take her to school, whom she could not tuck up at night, nor prepare Santa Claus surprises for her, and taste that sweetest of all joys, that of seeing a little face beam with delight. The child had been robbed of everything, and so had she. What an unending atonement! She had a child which she could not take into her own home. He felt that it was only now that he knew her really, and in spite of all the bitterness which filled his heart he sighed: "Poor Magda!" Magda had a child! Hron suddenly stopped dead; his thoughts glanced off in another direction. She *had* a child!

Ivan Hron took off his hat, wiped his forehead and looked straight in front of him at the green field. But he did not know what he was looking at, he was looking inwards. All the morbid moments of his brooding on the problem of their childlessness passed before his soul. He remembered how he had tormented himself to find the cause of it. And his wife had had... she had a child!

He stood, drawing deep breaths.

What was passing in Magda's mind, if she saw through him? Did she guess that he suspected the fault to be hers? And she had to bear the blame in silence.

He was overcome by remorse. He now realised fully how difficult the moment of their meeting would be.

Ivan Hron started off again along the edge of the field; he did not care whither he was going, he only sought for an escape from the labyrinth of his thoughts. He counted neither moments nor hours, he did not know how long he had been wandering about, when the setting sun reminded him that night was approaching.

He turned back towards Prague hurriedly, without minding by which road he went, noticing nothing by the way. From the Belvedere he turned to cross the Francis-Joseph bridge.

Not till he had reached the narrow Elisabeth Street did he become conscious of ordinary daily life again. He glanced at the two rows of high houses with their countless windows, and the thought struck him:

"Now, this is only a small fraction of a big town, yet what a multitude of little unimportant human beings, what life-stories, problems, emotions and struggles lie hidden behind all those windows, in all the rooms inhabited by people; under the roofs of the splendid mansions with balconies as well as under those of back-alleys. And when these struggling souls come out into the streets, they hide what is passing in them."

He was suddenly seized by a fear that some one might guess from his looks how miserable, humbled and desperate he felt. No! Only he himself should know what had happened to him; no one should stand still and look after him, pitying him and thinking: "Poor Hron, whatever is the matter with him?" As though he had not a trouble in the world, Hron pulled down his waistcoat, looked at his watch, felt whether he had a cigar with him, lit it deliberately, and walked towards Joseph's Square.

Along the narrow Elisabeth Street human life had flowed like a stream, but in Joseph Square it expanded in broad billows like a sea. All the excursionists converged hither to be scattered in all directions. The trams were rattling past, making the flag-stones tremble. Almost forgetting his troubles, he looked at the crowds which were storming the cars. These people, battling for room to sit or stand in them, seemed to him like lunatics. They fought their way with their elbows, pushed others off the steps to mount in their place; some positively butted into a medley of bodies and limbs, and others who had already boarded a car, were suddenly seized with fear and tried to alight again. Hats fell from their heads; some caught their dresses, and the seams of their garments were strained to the utmost, or gave way.

"What do they mean by it?" thought Hron, "why this wild struggle?"

The gas-lamps were beginning to sparkle... one... another... a third. Ivan Hron watched the lamplighter with his pole who went regularly from post to post with his head bent and without minding the wild tumult. A yellow mail-cart rattled past; the full letter boxes of the whole town would now yield their contents. Bourgeois with their wives returned from their walks; the women led the bigger children by the hand, the men carried the little ones. A detachment of firemen were crossing the street. The police were changing patrols.

Ivan felt that there was something restful to his mind in all this noise and movement, rattling and crowding. By degrees he became calmer. His senses, strained to breaking point by the great shock, relaxed and were able to take in other impressions. He put his hat, which had slipped back, straight and walked more firmly.

"Forget it all... at least for a while, for tonight!"

He made up his mind to join a party of his friends at a restaurant, so as to change his thoughts. He absolutely must think of something else, he had brooded enough. He meant to drink a good deal. Many people cure their troubles with wine; he too would try this remedy. He must avoid being alone in the empty house; he must take home an atmosphere of conviviality, else he would feel suffocated. And Hron went into a restaurant where he would be sure to meet friends.

But Ivan was one of those men who did not easily get drunk; his strong head could always master the effect of the wine, and he did not care to drink far beyond his measure. Yet the wine cheered him; he listened to the talk and gossip, and forced himself to join in. He spent several hours in this noisy company, and received his friends' respectful remembrances to his wife almost cheerfully. It was past midnight when he returned home. The servant was snoring in her bedroom next to the kitchen. Ivan gently locked the door and went through the hall on tiptoe. He found a letter from his wife on the table; she let him know by which train she intended to arrive. He lit the candles in his bedroom and went to bed with a book. But he had not been reading many lines when his hands with the book slowly dropped on the coverlet, and he looked across at the portrait of his wife over the chesterfield. For nearly an hour he lay quite still, looking fixedly at the lovely face which was so dear to him. He was painfully winning through to a resolution. Presently his lips moved without a sound, framing the words: "It shall be so." Perhaps he hardly heard them himself; he had instinctively given form to the last link in the chain of his thoughts, which might prove a solution of the problem.

Then he sat up in bed and put out both candles in the branch-candlestick. When he lay back in his pillows he whispered reproachfully: "Magda, Magda!"

FOUR

Magda Hron had told her husband that she would arrive on the last day of June by the afternoon train. Ivan was thankful that it would be in the later part of the day, almost in the evening; he would have the whole day to set his mind in order, as he said to himself.

He had hoped for this when he had returned from the restaurant the night before. But apparently the setting in order took him a shorter time than he had anticipated. Although he had been out unusually late the night before and had not gone to sleep for a good while, he awoke at an early hour and got up at once. He looked thoughtful but calm, his face betrayed no trace of yesterday's struggle. The storm had passed, his resolution held firm.

What was his resolution? Was he going to put his wife away? Or induce her to consent to a separation with maintenance for her and her daughter? This thought had occurred to him, but had been rejected at once. He realised that he could not hope to redeem his over-insistence in the past, nor ought to punish his wife by bringing an action. He was a prominent man, and his position would not stand a scandal; but apart from that, what would he gain by violent measures? Would he be the happier for them? Would they not utterly destroy

33

his future life? Was it likely that Magda would be happy, if the moment which restored her to her daughter were to rob her of her husband and home? And even if she should bear this fate without murmuring, could he live without her after the ten years of purest harmony between them, and when he loved her as much now as when he took her to his house for the first time? Nay... since yesterday he loved her with a passion which was mingled with pain; when he had learnt that he had a rival in the child, he had begun to tremble for his place in her heart.

FIVE

ron's struggle was over, he looked composed. He dressed quickly, breakfasted, and told the servant at what time her mistress would return, and what she was to prepare, lit his cigar and left the house. It was too early to go to his office, so he decided to go for a walk. A stroll without a set purpose on this warm, sunny morning of the departing June would strengthen today's resolution; he would breathe the fresh air, look at happy faces of people who went in all directions about their daily duties, taking them up at the point where they had left them yesterday, and trying not to show traces of intervening struggles.

He passed the Girls' High School. It was nearly eight o'clock, the children were hurrying to school. Many of them were accompanied by servants, elder sisters, or mothers. Hron stood still and from a distance watched the mothers taking leave of their darlings. They bent over them, gave them last instructions, then they kissed them lovingly and looked after them till they had disappeared in the school-entrance and winding corridors. His Magda would do the same; he knew she would not leave the child until she was quite sure she was safe. There was a faint smile on Hron's face when this thought crossed his mind like a flash. The stream of children was ebbing away: now it had been absorbed by the schoolhouse. Only a few late-comers ran in quickly, afraid of missing the beginning of the lesson; at last the place was completely deserted. Hron walked on towards his office.

The hours were all too slow for him that day. He could hardly wait for his wife's return. He went to the Sophia Island, to dine in company with a few friends whose families were already in the country.

"Still a grass-widower?" some of them asked him.

"Only till tonight," he answered with a smile, "my wife will return this afternoon from her visit to her parents; then it will be only a few days before we are off on our holiday somewhere. Our boxes are ready to be packed."

"Where are you going, Direktor?"

"Perhaps to Berlin and Hamburg on the way to Heligoland, or a quiet seaside place like Travemünde, perhaps in the other direction, to Munich, Salzburg and the Alpine Lakes. I don't know yet, I shall see what my wife proposes."

Hron was absent-minded at dinner and hurried away soon after, as though he were afraid to miss the train. He gulped down his cup of black coffee and went home. He opened the windows in his wife's room and in the dining-room, so that she should not find them stuffy on her return. He put a bunch of fresh flowers in the bedroom, carnations and roses, which he had bought on his way home. He locked her room, told the servant to have dinner ready at seven o'clock, and loitered towards his office, although the official hour had not yet struck, as though he could hurry on the clock. He could hardly contain himself.

But the nearer six o'clock and with it her arrival approached, the more uneasy he became, as if after all he dreaded their meeting. He was grateful to the chief cashier for joining him as far as the station when he left the Bank; he did not wish to be alone. And when the cashier had left him, he was drawn into a vortex of departing and arriving people; he felt dazed with the perpetual ringing of bells, shouting of the staff, thundering of trains which arrived from both directions. Yet he welcomed the infernal noise; it would sufficiently absorb Magda's senses not to make her look too closely at his features, and discover the emotion which had flushed his cheeks.

Then her train was signalled, and rolled into the station a few minutes later. He at once saw her, as she was alighting. A slight trembling seized him, a few steps brought him near to her. The blood mounted to her face. He was relieved that he had to turn and speak to a porter before addressing her. Magda took his arm and walked on quickly, almost drawing him forward; she was looking straight ahead. Her cheeks were almost on fire. Hron did not guess or understand that she too always suffered from great nervousness when she met him again for the first time. She was almost dying with fear that she might betray in some way whence she came and of what nature her visit had been. All her attention was fixed on guarding her secret, lest her husband should suspect her. But he had pressed her hand and drawn it closer… no, he suspected nothing! She was breathing more freely while he was helping her to get into the carriage, and while the wheels were rattling over the cobblestones. Saved once more!

"Well, Magda," said Hron, breaking the silence which had reigned between them since they had got into the carriage, and was beginning to frighten him, "have you had a good time? No disappointments?"

"Excellent, Ivan, everything went right," answered his wife.

"You find them all well?"

"Yes, quite. Father had not been well about a month ago. They did not tell me, because they did not want me to be anxious. But he is better, he is really quite well again."

"You found it hard to part with them, didn't you, Magda?" said Hron.

The blood again mounted to Magda's cheek. Her eyes became fixed, and did not meet his. Oh, how hard it had been to part with that little creature! But she was obliged to given an answer.

"You know I am fond of my parents, and they are getting old; every year is like a gift. And yet every year I leave them with the hope of seeing them the next."

"And they have not yet made up their minds to come and live in Prague?" he asked. "We could find a charming, cosy little nest for them and make them very comfortable. Haven't you tried to persuade them?"

Hron made this proposal every year on Magda's return from her old home, but she shrank from it. She would indeed have liked to have her parents near her, but if they came to Prague, how could she see little Magda? What pretext could she find? Two kinds of love were ever struggling within her, but the stronger, the mother-love always won the day.

"You are so kind, Ivan," she answered, "but I don't think we shall persuade them. They are too old; they had better stay in the surroundings in which they have lived all their lives; they would hardly get used to life in Prague. If anything happened to them they would be sure to think it was because they had left their old home. Besides, it would mean greater expense for you; as it is you are showing them so much kindness that I don't know how I can ever be grateful enough to you."

She warmly pressed his hand.

Ivan Hron was unspeakably happy. He kept her hand in his and said gently: "Be fond of me always, Magda. It is the sweetest gratitude you can give me."

They were both silent after that for the few minutes which it took to reach their home.

SIX

Two days later the couple left Prague. Ivan was restless, but not because he wanted a change of scene. He was almost unwilling to travel this year, indeed, quite unwilling. He would have liked to have carried out his plan at once, but he could not think of a cogent reason to give to his wife for not going for their usual trip. It was too late to pretend that he could not get leave; everything had been settled and prepared before Magda started to go to her parents. And Magda knew how he loved to travel. So they started, and went as far as Munich.

Hron was hoping that in strange surroundings, away from the daily round, and among strangers, he might more easily find an opportunity of saying what he wanted to say. On their travels, when they were closer companions than usual, they were always more tender, more intimate than at home. Hron always felt as though they were lovers.

The opportunity for which he was longing presented itself earlier than he thought. They stayed in Munich for a week, and went for a trip on the Stahrenberg Lake on their last day. It was a lovely, sunny morning. A light breeze was rippling the surface of the lake, when they left the train at Stahrenberg, to board the comfortable steamer "Wittelsbach". Their first objective was charming Leoni, where they ascended to the Rottmann's Height, and enjoyed the lovely view over the distant Alps. After an hour and a half they returned to the landing-stage, to go further up the lake by another steamer. A small family, perhaps belonging to the villa-colony of Leoni, boarded the steamer "Bavaria" at the same time; they were a young couple with two children, a boy of about three, a curly, sunburnt, restless little rogue, who ran about the deck like quicksilver, and a pale, almost transparent-looking girl of five, who was very much muffled up. It was easy to guess that this child with waxen cheeks had been racked by a severe illness quite recently, in fact, it had apparently not yet quite relaxed its hold upon the victim. The boy was looked after by a handsome, careful young girl but the mother herself was nursing her little daughter, happy at being able to take her out on the lake again for the first time. She hardly took her eyes off the precious convalescent, at whose bed, no doubt, she had watched for whole nights with bitter tears and fervent prayers.

With her tired, hollow eyes the little girl was looking at the lake, beneath the opalescent surface of which slumbered the green depth. They were fixed on one spot, as though she were expecting to see mermaids rising from the water; she knew them well, and mother had often told her the story. Now and then the child coughed, and then the young mother would cover her throat more closely with the silk handkerchief, or wrap the small, pointed elbows round with a cloak. And a kiss would accompany each of these movements.

Ivan Hron was watching his wife… her eyes had been resting for a long time on the little girl, and returned to her over and over again. Ivan read what was passing in her mind: "She is thinking of her little one."

41

The lovely morning, the fresh strong air, the view of the distant Alps had attuned his soul to tenderness; he was more receptive, more sensitive than usual. He guessed his wife's thoughts: yes, she is thinking of her child. Her little Magda too might be taken with a severe illness, might be wracked by fever. In her delirium she would call for her mother. Yet not her soft hand but a stranger's would minister to her; her mother dare not come. Perhaps in her last battle with death her dim eyes would be half opened to seek those she had loved above all things, her hands would be stretched out to embrace the head whose first and last thought was for her child... in vain, in vain! And her last dying groan would be wrung from her by the pain that her little heart could not break at her mother's breast.

Ivan Hron's eyes grew dim at this thought, and as though their thoughts had met, he heard a deep sigh which rose from his wife's bosom.

He took her hand. "You are looking at that poor child, Magda, you are sorry for her..."

His wife did not answer; her eyes looked into vacancy, her eyelids trembled.

"Yet how happy this child is, all the same," Ivan continued almost in a whisper. "She is carefully nursed, her mother watches her like a guardian angel."

Two large tears ran down Magdalena's cheeks; she had not the courage to look at her husband.

"Listen, Magda," said Ivan, taking her hand, "it has long been my intention to tell you something; there are so many orphans who do not belong to a soul in this world, who are in want of what they most need, and do not know what it means to be really loved and cared for. And as we ourselves have not been so fortunate as to have a family of our own, and we have no

42

children to consider, could we no adopt one of those lonely children who have no home? And it would be more lively for us, Magda…"

Magda did not answer; but the heaving of her breast showed the deep emotion in her soul, and what a storm of thoughts and conflicts her husband's words had roused.

"You do not answer, Magda, you do not agree? You do not care about it?"

"Do as you wish." Her words were almost inaudible.

"Ah, I knew you would not thwart me, Magda," said Ivan gently. "And if you should be thinking about your people, believe me, in case I should die unexpectedly no one will be curtailed by this increase in our family. I have made provisions for everybody as well as you. Look," he continued eagerly, "some little boy who has neither father nor mother shall find them in us. Would you like me to look out for a curly little fellow like this one?"

Magda's hand was trembling in his. "As you like, Ivan; yes, I agree."

Ivan was silent, then he began again: "Or would you rather have a little girl? A little creature whose mind would begin to open out when she lived with us; she would soon get used to us and would see her parents in us… we could give her our names. You'd rather have a girl, wouldn't you, Magda? A girl is more domesticated; you could dress her, and make of her what you liked, give her mind its proper bent… yes, I think you would get more quickly used to a girl, wouldn't you?"

The young woman's eyes looked glassy, although the two tears on her cheeks had dried, but a fresh pain which would have no end was beginning to take possession of her soul. Her fixed eyes, unable to perceive anything in her immediate surroundings, looked into the far distance, and her heard went out in immeasurable sorrow, hunted to death. If ever she had dared to hope that the day might come when she could acknowledge little Magda, if ever a ray of hope had lighted up her soul… all that would be lost now. What she had felt for her own, what she would have done for her with her last breath, was now to be given to an unknown child. The place which she had dreamt of for the unfortunate little creature would never be taken by her. Oh, the pain of it! The awful punishment for a single moment of weakness, the endless atonement for the sin of another! Her Magda would now really be lost to her; she would for ever be excluded from her rightful place.

The thought of humbling herself before her husband and revealing her secret, flashed through her mind. But she forced it away from her. Should she, at the moment when he was thinking of doing good and giving a home and parents to some unfortunate being, crush him with her dreadful disclosure?

After a long pause, and without looking at him: "Yes, do so," she said in a whisper.

"You really mean it, and you don't even look at me?" said Hron as with a gentle reproach. "I know it is hard to speak of these things, but I am afraid there is no prospect of a change. But all the same, if you do not like the idea…"

When later on Magda remembered this moment, she was conscious of having fought a hard battle with herself for the second time in her life, just as hard as that after which she had consented to accept Ivan's hand. But now she had the strength to turn to him, and look at him with her brimming eyes, while her hand gently returned the pressure of his right hand. She said firmly: "Not at all, I quite agree with you."

The subject was not mentioned between them again. The day

was bright, and everything looked smiling, the rays of July sun shone warm upon them, but they remained silent all day. The deep melancholy which had taken possession of her could not be banished from Magda's face. Hron at first tried to distract her, but ended by being lost in silent reflection too. For him also this afternoon's conversation had meant a hard struggle. He had prepared himself for many days, and every time he had meant to begin, the words had stuck in his throat. But in spite of his serious mood, he had a feeling of deep satisfaction, and if he had been a more introspective man, he would have said to himself that he was really immensely happy.

After this conversation with his wife, Ivan became restless. He shortened the remainder of their trip, hurried from place to place, and left unvisited some in which he had meant to make a stay. He often secretly watched Magda, and saw how she was suffering. She mastered herself with all her strength, tried to conquer the apprehension which Ivan's intention had roused in her, and even made attempts to appear gay. Perhaps she secretly clung to the hope that something would prevent the plan at the last moment. But how could that be? She could not tell. If she were to change his mind in favour of her daughter, she would have to speak. Could that change possibly be in her child's and her own favour? Might she not be sent away with her unfortunate child at once? She could do nothing. And Ivan, who read her thoughts, became himself subject to depression. His nature, more robust than hers, was not affected as deeply as her sensitive soul, yet he became more and more anxious to put an end to this state of uncertainty. The solution of the problem was in his hand, and he fervently desired to solve it; yet when he thought of what it would mean, he trembled for Magda and for himself.

In Salzburg rainy weather set in, which gave him a pretext for returning to Prague without delay. Magda did not seem to care what they did; nothing had appealed to her on this journey, neither did she look forward to going home. Dull indifference had now taken possession of her. What did it matter whether she were away or at home? The situation was desperate in any case. There was no way out of the impasse. She strained all her senses to get hold of an idea, but none presented itself; not a single flash came to light up the heavy gloom of her horizon.

They were home again. Ivan Hron's leave had not yet expired. He went to his office to see whether there were news of any importance, but after he had settled that he need not resume his duties for another fortnight, he returned to his wife. On the next day he made preparations for another journey. "I have to attend to some business in the country, Magda," he said, "I want to settle it while I am on leave. But I shall be back in a couple of days or so, and if you like we can then go for another trip. Perhaps a favourable wind may blow me in the direction of your home. I may see your parents; but I am not sure."

When he took leave of her, with his bag in his hand, he remarked casually: "Well, Magda, if I should find a little orphan by the wayside, you would not mind my bringing her along? It would be best to get one from the country; all her former ties, whatever they might be, would then be severed, and she would begin a new life in Prague. If you should not take to her, we will send her back."

"Do as you think best," said Magda with resignation. "I am sure I shall approve of your choice; you are a man who can be trusted."

"If I succeed, I will write and let you know," said Hron, tenderly embracing his wife, and left the house.

Three days passed. Hron had not written. But on the morning of the fourth day she received a letter:

"Dearest Magda, – I have found what I was looking for, a little girl without father and mother. She is not quite so small a child as you might fancy, but I hope you will take to her all the same. Meet us the day after tomorrow at the North Western Station at 1 P.M. Be sure to have dinner ready at once; we shall probably be hungry. Greatly looking forward to our meeting – Your IVAN"

SEVEN

Magda went towards the station to meet her husband, with a heavy heart. She walked up and down the platform, and her breath stopped when she heard the whistle of the approaching train. Immovable, as though she were rooted to the spot, the young woman stood, her eyes only were moving and wandered from one carriage to another, seeking the one from which her husband would alight with the child. But the passengers, each one looking for friends or relatives who would meet them, passed her; one carriage after another discharged its occupants, and at last the train was empty; the doors stood out like wooden wings, the engine hissed feebly. Ivan was nowhere to be seen. He had not come.

Magda stood a little while longer, waiting to see if her husband would appear after all; at last she wondered whether she had made a mistake in the time. Having asked some questions of uncommunicative officials, which were not answered any too willingly, she returned home. The thought that something might have happened to her husband did not occur to her. She thought that she might not have read his note carefully enough, or that he had made a mistake in the time. Besides, she was too much engrossed in other things. Her thoughts were far away in a remote little village in the North-east of Bohemia with her

Magda… her Magda who did not know that her place would now be taken by another child.

Magda had gone up the front door steps of her house and was pressing the electric bell.

How lonely the house had felt while Ivan had been away!

The door was opened at once, and… by Ivan himself. She was taken aback, almost startled, so that he had to draw her into the hall. He kissed her and said: "You have had the trouble for nothing, Magda, forgive me. I altered my plans at the last moment, and we came by the main line. There was no time to let you know, so I was obliged to let you take a walk by yourself. But come in now, come and see…"

"*We* came? Then she is here!"

Suddenly Magda's feet refused to move; she tried in vain to follow her husband. He gently put his arm around her shoulders and led her, so that she was obliged to move forward. Half-leading, half-drawing her, he took her as far as the dining-room door which he opened. When he spoke encouragingly to her once more, there was a slight tremor in his voice. "Come now, Magda," he said, "come and tell me if you are pleased with me." He pushed her gently forward without releasing his hold upon her.

Magda looked into the room, where a shy little girl was sitting on the sofa. She looked startled, and perhaps a little frightened after all the changes she had lived through during the last two days. Her large brown eyes were looking towards the door when she heard the voice of the man whose she had only so lately met for the first time. But when she saw Magda appear on the threshold, she sprang to her feet, her cheeks burned, and she cried: "Mummy!"

"Magda!"

Magdalena's voice choked, the last syllable remained un-spoken. The blood left her face, her body was swaying. She clutched the fingers of Ivan's right hand as though she were drowning; still she could not stand, and sank down on her knees which had given way beneath her.

"Magda," cried Hron, trying to hold her up, "pull yourself together, little mother."

Magda resisted. Not standing… only kneeling could she listen to the terrible things which a deceived husband must now speak.

But his arms lifted her up completely, and his right hand raised her head which had dropped onto her chest.

"Magda," he whispered, trembling all over, "be brave, don't frighten our little daughter."

He lifted her head almost by force, to look into her eyes. But she had closed them, a deathly pallor had spread over her face, her teeth were chattering as if in a fever. She could hardly utter the words: "Who told you, Ivan, who told you?"

'Nobody told me." Hron passed his hand over her cold cheek. "I want you to be perfectly happy, my dearest child. Now, please go and welcome the other Magda, else she will begin to cry. Come little daughter, give your mother courage."

The child hesitated for a moment, then she ran up to her mother, threw her arms around her body, and cried anxiously: "Mummy, Mummy, what is the matter with you?"

But Magda, before Ivan knew what she was doing, or could prevent it, had seized his right hand and pressed it to her lips. It was not till now that the truth flashed upon her. Ivan had brought this about, but not to accuse or punish her. Hot tears fell on his hands, and when at last he could take her head in both his hands to kiss her, her whole soul looked in gratitude out of her brimming eyes.

50

"Ivan... Ivan," her lips trembled, "do you think my whole life will be enough in return for what you are doing for this fatherless child?"

"What? Fatherless!" Ivan cried gaily, so as not to break down himself, "she has had a father for two whole days... he has been found, he has come to claim her, here is documentary evidence... look here."

He put his hand in his breast pocket, drew forth a document and waved it over her head: "While I was about it I have bought Magda's christening certificate as well, so now we can enter her at the High School after the holidays. But enough of all this. The poor little thing is waiting to be kissed!"

In a moment the little girl was buried in her mother's arms.

Ivan looked with infinite love at his wife, whose face had suddenly grown crimson. After a little while he said: "Now, little woman, give the child something to eat, I believe she is famished. And after dinner you had better get her some clothes that she is fit to be seen in in a town... how nice it will be to have something to be busy about! And tomorrow, or the day after, we will go right away from Prague once more, and get used to our little family in some pretty hiding-place."

THE END

VERY SHORT CLASSICS

This book is part of the 'Very Short Classics' series, a collection of short books from around the world and across the centuries, many of which are being made available as ebooks and paperbacks for the very first time.

Also available in the Very Short Classics series...

THE FOUR DEVILS by Herman Bang

When their mother drowns, young brothers Fritz and Adolf are sold into the circus by their grandmother, for a mere twenty marks. There they suffer under the cruel hand of Father Cecchi but are befriended by sisters Aimée and Louise and together they create an acrobatic act.

When Cecchi dies and the circus disbands, the quartet find there is little demand for acrobats and they refine their skills, re-emerging at The Four Devils, death-defying trapeze artists. Soon they are the talk of Europe, flying high from one city to another.

But one of the Four Devils, Aimée, finds that her feelings for Fritz have outgrown that of a sibling love and become a passion that pervades her every waking moment. So when

Fritz begins an affair with an aristocratic heiress, Aimée's heart is broken and tensions threaten to also break the Four Devils apart, forever.

The Four Devils is a short novella from one of Denmark's most acclaimed writers.

SOUVENIRS OF FRANCE by Rudyard Kipling

'Sixty pages... of memory, praise, nostalgia and gratitude' Julian Barnes

Rudyard Kipling's love affair with India is well-documented but his affection for France and its people is less well-known. It started at the age of twelve when he would regularly accompany his father to the Paris Exhibition of 1878, where the elder Kipling was in charge of the Indian Section of Arts and Manufactures. Young Rudyard would be sent off in the morning with two francs in his pocket and instructions to stay out of trouble. He would spend his money on 'satisfying déjeuners' and 'celestial gingerbreads' as well as frequent trips up inside the head of the Statue of Liberty, then part of the Exhibition prior to being shipped to Ellis Island.

He returned to France a decade later, as a young man, and then regularly in the years that followed, sometimes for pleasure, sometimes on business – such as when working for the British Imperial War Graves Commission. He was a frequent visitor for the rest of his life.

Souvenirs of France was originally published in 1933, and was one of the last of Kipling's books to appear during his lifetime. It is a very personal and fascinating portrait of a great writer and of a country that had a special place in his heart.

Printed in Great Britain
by Amazon